Merci à Lucie et Michel — C.A.
For Orrine and Marla, treasure hunters extraordinaire! — A.C.

Owlkids Books acknowledges the financial support of the Canada Council for the Arts, the Ontario Arts Council, the Government of Canada through the Canada Book Fund (CBF), and the Government of Ontario through the Ontario Creates Book Initiative for our publishing activities.

Published in Canada by
Owlkids Books Inc.
1 Eglinton Avenue East
Toronto, ON M4P 3A1

Published in the United States by
Owlkids Books Inc.
1700 Fourth Street
Berkeley, CA 94710

Catalogage avant publication de Bibliothèque et Archives Canada

Titre: Dragon! : a story told in two languages / written by Caroline Adderson ; illustrations by
Alice Carter = Dragon! : une histoire racontée en deux langues / texte de Caroline Adderson ; illustré par Alice Carter.
Noms: Adderson, Caroline, 1963- auteur. | Carter, Alice, 1977- illustrateur. | Adderson, Caroline, 1963- Dragon! |
Adderson, Caroline, 1963- Dragon! Français.
Description: Mention de collection: Pierre & Paul ; 2 | Texte en anglais et en français.
Identifiants: Canadiana 20200274708F | ISBN 9781771473286 (couverture rigide)
Classification: LCC PS8551.D3267 D73 2021 | CDD jC813/.54—dc23

Library and Archives Canada Cataloguing in Publication

Title: Dragon! : a story told in two languages / written by Caroline Adderson ; illustrations by
Alice Carter = Dragon! : une histoire racontée en deux langues / texte de Caroline Adderson ; illustré par Alice Carter.
Names: Adderson, Caroline, 1963- author. | Carter, Alice, illustrator. | Adderson, Caroline, 1963-
. Dragon! | Adderson, Caroline, 1963- Dragon! French.
Description: Series statement: Pierre & Paul ; 2 | Text in English and French.
Identifiers: Canadiana 20200274708E | ISBN 9781771473286 (hardcover)
Classification: LCC PS8551.D3267 D73 2021 | DDC jC813/.54—dc23

Library of Congress Control Number: 2020939438

Edited by Karen Li and Stacey Roderick | Designed by Jill Monsod

Manufactured in Guangzhou, Dongguan, China, in September 2021, by Toppan Leefung Packaging & Printing
(Dongguan) Co., Ltd.   Job #BAYDC76/R1

B   C   D   E   F   G

MIX
Paper from
responsible sources
FSC® C104723

ONTARIO ARTS COUNCIL
CONSEIL DES ARTS DE L'ONTARIO
an Ontario government agency
un organisme du gouvernement de l'Ontario

Canada Council
for the Arts

Conseil des Arts
du Canada

Canada

Publisher of Chirp, Chickadee and OWL
www.owlkidsbooks.com

Owlkids Books is a division of bayard canada

PIERRE & PAUL
DRAGON!

A story told in two languages
Une histoire racontée en deux langues

WRITTEN BY/TEXTE DE
CAROLINE ADDERSON

ILLUSTRATED BY/ILLUSTRÉ PAR
ALICE CARTER

OWLKIDS BOOKS

Paul and Pierre are great explorers.

Ils sont aussi des amis.

Friends and explorers.

Aujourd'hui, ils sont des chasseurs de trésor.

They draw a treasure map.

Le père de Paul entre.

"Paul, what day is it?"

«C'est jeudi », dit Pierre.

"Thursday?" Paul looks up. "Garbage day!"

« Oui ! dit Pierre. Allons-y ! »

Les chasseurs de trésor partent en voyage.

They take out their map.

Suddenly they hear a roar.

Un *grand* rugissement!

Treasure hunters are always prepared.

Ils prennent leurs armes.

sword

bouclier

shield

épée

The battle begins.

C'est une *grande* bataille.

« Es-tu mort ? »
demande Pierre.

"Yes, I'm dead."

Quelqu'un arrive.

"What happened here?" asks the man.

« Il est mort »,
répond Pierre.

"Come on, Princess,"
the man says.

"What!" cries the man. "Dead?"

Le chien lèche Paul.

Paul sits up. "Hey!"

Pierre dit : « Il est vivant ! »

Paul asks, "Where are we?"

« Nous sommes ici, dit Pierre. Au marais empoisonné. »

"A poisonous swamp?" Paul sniffs. "No wonder it stinks."

Pierre renifle l'air aussi. «Oui, ça pue. Sortons d'ici !»

The treasure hunters race knee-deep through the poisonous swamp, dodging snapping crocodiles.

Ils traversent la forêt épineuse.

Enfin, ils sont arrivés à la mer.

«Arrête!» crie Pierre.

"Is this it?" Paul asks. "The treasure?"

« Non, c'est un bateau ! »

"A boat?"

lampshade
abat-jour

CE CÔTÉ VERS LE HAUT

umbrella
parapluie

books
livres

skateboard
planche
à roulettes

Pierre monte dans le bateau.
« Voilà ! »

Paul gives him a captain's hat.
He gives him two paddles. "Ta-da!"

des pagaies

chapeau
de capitaine

« Moi, je suis capitaine, dit Pierre. Et toi ? »

"I'm the ocean,"
says Paul.

Soudain, Pierre entend un bruit épouvantable.

Paul hears the terrible noise, too.

Les deux explorateurs nagent.

They swim to shore and run for it.

«Où sommes-nous?» demande Pierre.

"Where's the map?" Paul asks.

« La carte ! » crie Pierre.

"The treasure!" cries Paul. "Now we'll never find it!"

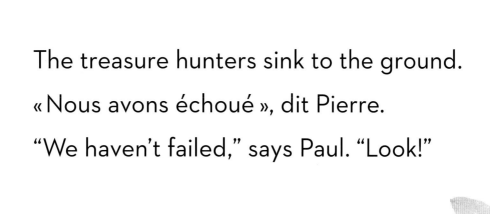

The treasure hunters sink to the ground.

« Nous avons échoué », dit Pierre.

"We haven't failed," says Paul. "Look!"

Le père de Paul les attend à la maison.

"Where were you?" he asks.

"Treasure hunting," Paul says.

"I thought you were taking out the garbage," Dad says.

«Regardez!» dit Pierre.

"One person's trash is another person's treasure," Paul's dad says.

Les explorateurs ne répondent pas.

They're off treasure hunting again.